T0380903

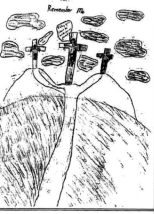

Stories

Through

Different

Eyes

Illustrated and Written

By

Michael John Lowe

To order additional copies of this book, contact:
Xlibris
1-888-795-4274
www.Xlibris.com
Orders@Xlibris.com

ISBN: 978-1-7960-6935-8 (sc)
ISBN: 978-1-7960-6936-5 (hc)
ISBN: 978-1-7960-6934-1 (e)

Library of Congress Control Number: 2018900654

Print information available on the last page.

Rev. date: 10/30/2019

STORIES THROUGH DIFFERENT EYES

Illustrated and Written

By

Michael John Lowe

TABLE OF CONTENTS

The Innkeeper's Story

THE INN KEEPER'S STORY

Hello, I'm just another inn keeper in a little city called Bethlehem, but my story is beyond words.

The week had been so chaotic, and mysterious. Why was this year so different? One of the peculiar things about the week was a star. You might ask, "Why a star? Stars are in the sky every night." You are correct, but this star was so bright, and more than that, it also shined during the day. A simple star, was there a purpose for such a spectacle? Then there was the wild and craziness of my city which I saw every year at this time, for you see, people from many regions had to come back to their homelands to pay their taxes, something no one enjoyed doing. Now, as you might expect, I was exhausted at the end of each day, and when I closed my doors to the inn each night, sleep could not come soon enough.

As was my custom each night when I still had rooms available. I left my lamp in the window. Perhaps, due to fatigue, I forgot to take my lamp out of the window, for on this night I had sold all my rooms. This time of year was very dear to me since this was when I made the most money, but still it always bothered me when I had to tum people away.

It was late, I was sound asleep. When I heard what sounded like someone knocking on my door. Who were these people? Could they not see the inn was closed? Knock! Knock! Knock! The knocking did not stop, so I got up and went to the door, and it was then that I realized that I had not taken the lamp out of the window. I opened the door knowing that I would have to give them the bad news that I had no more rooms. There in front of me stood a young couple. And to make matters worse, the woman was pregnant. I thought she was going to have the baby right there. My heart sank as I had to tell them that I had no more rooms, but what could I do? The man spoke first. "Surely you still have one room left; after all, your lamp is still in the window." "I know," I said, "I am sorry, but I was so tired I forgot to take my lamp out of my window," and then the woman spoke softly. "Please sir, we have traveled for over a day and we are also tired, and I am afraid that tonight may be the night that my son is bom. Don't you have anything we can just lay down and rest in?"

My heart was broken. Of all the people to leave out in the cold! I gazed up into the sky, as if to say, what can I do? It was at that moment that I saw the star that had been shining so brightly this past week, and I thought to myself, I do have a stable out back, and there is some hay that can be like a bed just for the night. So I offered them my stable. It was not much, but at least it was a shelter, and the star was so bright there would be plenty of light. "Thank you!

Thank you!" the couple exclaimed, "we will make it right with whatever we owe you in the morning, thank you!" There were no words for me to say, this couple was truly unique. Who else would accept a stable to sleep in, especially being pregnant? "No charge," was all I could muster up to say, after all, could you charge someone to sleep in a stable with the likes of cows, donkeys, sheep, and probable chickens?

The next morning I woke up at the crack of dawn, for I had slept restlessly worrying about that young couple out in the stable. I got dressed and ran into the stable to see how they were, and there was the baby. He was so precious just lying there sleeping with his mother and father. I just stood there in awe, the animals seemed to be singing softly to the baby. "Moo,", "Bah" went the cows and the sheep, and as if the rooster knew the hard night this little family had the night before, not a sound did he make as if to say, "Rest, sleep well." I went back into the inn and just pondered what I had just witnessed.

In the days to come, people from kings to peasants came to see the baby. I noticed that the star that had been ever present for so long was no longer present. Who was this child? Was the star there to point the way to this baby? Perhaps. But why? Why were so many drawn to my little stable?

As I reflect back on that night, it truly was one of mystery and awe. When I found out who this child was and what He would do for this world, I was amazed that He came into the world in the humblest of ways, but He would leave this world as the greatest man who ever lived. After all is said and done, I, being just an inn keeper, learned to be willing to give all that I had, and as a result I was rewarded for life. It was with no expectations that I gave all that I had, but I can tell you I received the greatest gift of my life on that night so long ago.

Ten Touched

One Returns

TEN TOUCHED, ONE RETURNS

It was a day I shall never forget. Nine others and myself left our community in pursuit of the one they called "The Healer".

Let me tell you a little about myself and my life. I was born into a wonderful family of four, although I rarely see them anymore after all these years, for you see, I have this terrible di3sease which prohibits me from living with my family. I remember the day my family went out into the community for the first time. It was a long sad journey for our family. My mother and sister were in tears most of the way, with my mother asking my father, "Why do we have to do this to our son, is there not another way?" My father, fighting back tears of his own, while trying to be strong, replied, "This is the way it must be, he cannot stay with us in town, for the town will surely throw him out into the wild, and let him die if we don"t do this now, I want our son to live."

After what seemed more than just an hour, we arrived at where I would call my new home for many years to come. My father went to the leader of the community and said, "Here is my son, will you please take care of him?"

"Yes sir," was the leader"s reply, and with that, my family returned home without me. I screamed, Come back! Come back, crying so loud the heavens could hear me, but on they went without me. The only sound louder than my own, was my mother"s crying and groaning. That was the saddest day for many years to come. Now, after a few weeks had passed, reality set in. I was here to stay, and this was my new family. It became a family of love, but I must tell you, a real blood family's love never goes away. I still always yearned for my real family. By now I was about thirteen years old, and the leader asked me to go into town for supplies. He told me I was now old enough to make the journey on my own, and the town would not hassle me as a boy, as much as they would the elders of the community. Up until this time, I had not known why my family had brought me here, but I would soon find out.

I thanked the leader of the community for believing in me to do this job. I got my donkey, and we left for town. This would be the first of many trips I would make over the years, and perhaps the hardest. As I came into town on this day, I could feel the sense that I was being stared at, and kind of mocked, but why? What had I done? I guess on this trip I was lucky because the merchants let me purchase my supplies, but as I left town, they yelled for me never to come back. In the weeks and years to come, I actually had to disguise myself to get into town and get as many supplies as I could before they recognized me and threw me out yelling, "Get out! Get out, and never come back!" The trips to town never got easier, just harder, but I still went. One day while I was in town,

I heard about a man coming into town who could heal all people of their diseases. All the way home, I pondered if this man could be for real. Could he heal all of our diseases? I thought about this all week long.

The next weekend's journey day finally came, and I was so excited, for this was to be the day I would try to meet this man who was said to be able to heal all people. I gathered up nine of my best friends, and off to town we went to meet this man.

Now, as we approached the town gate, we could see a large crowd gathered together. Could this be him? Could this really be the man who could heal us? We entered the gate so excited, we felt like we could jump right out of our skin. Then the town people recognized me and my friends and started shouting, "Get out! Get out! Go back to where you came from, you don't belong here! You are unclean, go home now!" Our excitement turned into utter sadness, that is until we heard him speak. His voice was soothing as he spoke to the people and told them, "I am come to heal all people, let this man come to me with his friends." The crowd suddenly silenced, so much so that you could have heard a coin drop on the dirt. Stunned, my friends and I walked hesitantly towards him. Could he, or would he heal my friends and I as we had heard? When we got up to him, he gave us some instructions to follow, and said we would be healed. In all the excitement, I cannot remember what he told us to do, I just know that whatever they were, my friends and I did them, and we were healed! We jumped for joy, yelling and screaming, We are healed! We are healed. Our spots are gone! Our friends watched in utter amazement, it truly was a miracle. My friends and I ran off with joy, each of us in our own direction.

As I was running off to find my real family to show them what this man had done, I stopped dead in my tracks. I had not thanked this man for healing me. When I got to him, I fell on my knees and thanked him over and over again. I was so overcome with joy. I just knelt there and sobbed. As he spoke, he touched me, and my body just trembled. "Sir, he said, were there not ten of you whom I healed, where are the other nine?" Sir, I do not know. All I know is that you healed me, and that I had to come back and say thank you. With tears running down my face, I looked into his eyes as he said, "Go, your faith has made you well." Whoever this man was, I may never know. All I know is that he healed me. I never saw the other nine friends who were healed with me again. I often wonder if they came back and thanked this man as I had. All I know is that he healed me, and my life will never be the same.

WERE YOU THERE?

would like to take you on a journey back to the first Holy Week. That week was such a strange week for me, and let me tell you why.

This week was a week that I, along with many of my friends, had anticipated for so long, because the city's son was finally coming home. I remember waking up at the dawn that Sunday morning so I could greet this man at the parade we had planned for him. Look! Look, I screamed, as I saw him approaching in the distance. He is here! Our son has come home! This man was expected to be the King of the .Jews. Soon everyone began to shout, "Hosanna! Hosanna! Hosanna to the King of the .Jews! The sound was deafening. The people threw their cloaks and palm branches on the ground for him, after all, he was a king right? Can you imagine my surprise when this so called king came riding in on a donkey, the lowest form of transportation of all in that day? I was very confused to say the least, was this not the king we expected, or was he still to come? What a way to start my week, in one day I had gone from shear joy, and by the end of the day, a feeling of being let down, and by the end of the week, my friends and I would not believe what we would see. We would see betrayal, denial, death, and finally salvation.

The next few days were feelings of rejection, for we had not gotten the king we expected, but the leaders of the city were still upset at the attention this man was getting, so they started plotting to kill this man, but they did not know how to get to him. Then they saw me, and how disappointed I looked, and they picked up on my emotions. Knowing that I was one of this man's best friends, they approached me with some silver coins, and asked me to show them to this man in the crowd, at a time I was at my lowest, all I had to do was kiss this man's cheek. It did not dawn on me until I was sitting next to him at supper, what I had done. My friend spoke to all of us at the table and said, "Tonight one of you will betray me." Now the eleven friends I was with began to ask, " Is it I Lord, is it I?" My leader turned to me and replied, "He whose cup I dip my bread in will betray me," and then it happened. It was my cup, and shortly after that I left the room, and did in fact deliver the kiss, and received the coins. What had I done? Take it back! Take it back! I yelled, but the deed had been done. I no longer had a reason to live, so I took my life. This was the beginning of the end for our leader. After supper we were all exhausted, but our leader knew what was coming, so he asked us to join him in the garden called Gethsemane to pray. He left us there and went to another part of the garden to pray alone. Some time had passed and our leader came back to find us all fast asleep. "Could you not pray with me for just a little while?" he asked. We were all so ashamed, but we had a long day, and we could just not stay awake. The next day for me, Peter, was the worst day of my life. Our leader had told me that I would deny three times before the rooster crowed, and 1, being the one who I thought was his favorite, boldly and strongly rebuked him saying, "I love you, I will never deny you!" Before I knew it, I had been approached three different times and accused of knowing this man, and fearing for my life, I emphatically said not once, but three times, "I do not know him". "Cock-a-doodle-doo!" went the rooster, and then I remembered our leaders words. How could I have done this? I was supposed to be his friend.

By now our leader had been captured by the soldiers, and taken to the ruler of the land for trial. Five days ago I had been chanting, "Hosanna, King of the Jews," and now when the ruler proclaimed that he saw no evidence to convict this man, and turned it over to me and the crowd around me to pronounce sentence on this man, we had two choices. A known murderer, or our leader, who we did not even know had done anything wrong, but I got wrapped up in the crowd as we chose our leader to be crucified over a true murderer. "Crucify him! Crucify him!" we chanted, and so it was done. Our leader was sentenced to die on a cross. We followed our leader as he carried the heavy cross by himself, to the top of the hill, and watched as they nailed him to the cross.

There were now three crosses on the hill, two of us I knew were guilty, but this man in the middle, I did not understand. I had watched him do miraculous things from my jail window all week, and all I saw in him was compassion for others. Why was he hanging next to me? From what I had seen this week, I knew he was special, and for whatever reason, I felt like he could do a miracle for me right now, so I asked him, "Will you remember me?" I cried as I heard his last words to his father. "Forgive them, for they know not what they do," and then he spoke to me and said, "Today, you will be with me in heaven," and I took my last breath.

Finally, 1, still weeping at the loss of this man three days before, returned to the tomb where he was buried. When I got to the tomb, I could not believe my eyes. The stone protecting the entrance was gone, and then I saw them, the Angel's who told me, "He is not here. He is Risen!" I, still confused and bewildered, walked away. As I was walking away, a man came up to me and asked what was wrong? I told him that the tomb where my savior was buried is now empty, and then he spoke my name, "Mary", and I knew it was him! He was alive! Two of his followers came running up to me and asked, "Where is he?" I told them, "He is Risen, He is Risen indeed.

This would be the first of many Easters to come. With Easter comes the gift of salvation, just for the asking. On that dark and agonizing Friday afternoon, you and I were given the opportunity to become new creatures, and become one in Christ, so that we might one day join Him in paradise.

Remember Me

When I was a child I had a loving family, one which anyone would have begged to have, but as is often the case, I did not know what I had until it was too late. My life was ruined until my final breath. Let me explain.

As I told you, I ruined my life. It was nobody's fault but my own. The family I had were pillars of stone holding me up to keep me straight and tall, but all my life I became a sponge, causing me to become weak. My family always supported me with good, positive things to build me up, but I could not see it at the time. I always chose the bad over my family's good. Why? I don't know.

Somehow as I was growing up, I was never satisfied with what I had. My father worked very hard to provide as best he could for his family, but did I appreciate it? NO! I did not understand his love until many years later as I hung on a cross, paying the price for my wrong doings. Up until that day, the grass was always greener on the next oasis, my friends all had camels, and all I had were my feet.

I began to steal at a young age, at first out of the innocence of a child, but instead of appreciating the help and support of my family, I rejected it, and did not learn from my actions as a child. My wrong doings just increased with age until I reached adulthood. Now, after all these years, my family could no longer cover for me. I was on my own. What a disappointment I had become to my family, but even after all I had done in my life, there was my family standing at the foot of the cross. Why were they here? How could they want to support me after all the trials I had put them through in my life? Were they there to mock me now? To say, "See? We told you so." I did not believe that was the case, but it was not until my final hour of life that I realized they were not there to mock me, but rather, to show that I was still loved.

I had now been imprisoned for what seemed like a lifetime, and my sentenced crucifixion was finally just a week away. It was now that reality finally kicked in within me, obviously by now it was way too late, but I decided to enjoy my last week of life as best I could. During this week I saw mol re than I had in my whole life, and I believe what I witnessed was what prepared me for my final day of life. How thankful I was that my jail cell had a window that I could look out into the city, and see all the things going on. This last week of my life was much different for me, but why? Why had this not happened before? In my final breath, I would finally know the answer.

Wow! I was suddenly drawn to my cell window from all the yelling and shouting going on in the streets. I looked out and saw what looked like a parade, but whoever this was for had to be very, very special because people were throwing palm branches, and even their coats on the road for this person. Then I heard all the people shouting, "Hosanna! Hosanna! The king of the Jews," and as I watched in anticipation of seeing a king come into town, I was shocked, for all I saw was a man riding into town on a donkey. Who was this man they called the king of the Jews? He was no different from me. I thought about all the times I had ridden into town on my donkey. Who was this man, was he really a king?

During the next few days, all I saw was this man being surrounded by people. He seemed to have something the people wanted or needed. This man seemed to be so loving and caring to all he met, and the only ones who did not respond to him were the leaders of the city. They seemed upset that this man was getting all the attention of the townspeople. From my cell window I saw this man continuing to love and care for all who would come to him. He seemed to good to be true. A perfect man, one who did no wrong. Well, my final day of life finally came. The guard woke me up early. I was fed better this morning than all the years I had been in prison, and with tears in my eyes him, and then I was escorted to a hilltop, and hung on a cross.

There were now two of us on our crosses on that hilltop, and we were just waiting until our death. Both myself and the other convict just hung there and cried. Whether it was for the fact that we were finally being put to death, or the pain we were enduring, the reason I didn"t know. Maybe it was a little of both.

By now, I was barely clinging to life, gasping for each breath of air, and then I saw him. It was like I had gotten a new breath of life. As I stated at this man coming up the hill, I could not believe my eyes, it was the man I had watched all week. What had happened in the last two days? This man in my eyes could do no wrong, so why was he coming up the hill carrying his own cross? The other thief and myself did not have to carry our own crosses. I truly was confused, not believing what I was seeing and hearing. Five days ago, all I heard was Hosanna, the king of the Jews, and now all I was hearing was Crucify him! Crucify him! What had happened? I watched in horror as they nailed him to the cross, hearing his agonizing groans with each nail driven into his hands and feet. Then his cross was placed between the two us.

Finally, I could contain myself no longer, I had to ask. Sir, why are you here? You have done no wrong. "Shut up!" the other thief gasping for air yelled. "Obviously, he like us, has to be punished." I did not believe him. I knew what I had seen this past week. I heard him beg for water, to which they gave him vinegar, and I heard his agonizing cry as they pierced his side with their spears, and then I heard him say, "Father, forgive them, for they know not what they do." It was then that I realized that this was no ordinary man, so for whatever reason, in my final breath, I asked him to remember me in heaven. He replied, "Your sins are forgiven, and today you shall be with me in paradise." I now saw why the people flocked to him as they did. I was now at peace as I took my last breath and went to sleep.

Is it You?

Is It You

The greatest man who ever lived, I was one of his twelve best friends. For many years I traveled with him, and witnessed many of the things he did to earn him the title of the greatest man who ever lived, but yet it was I who had to ask, is it you?

All my life I had been a skeptic, one who could not just hear something and believe it. I was like a scientist during my life, I always had to have proof of anything I heard. It was this attitude that earned me the name, "The Doubter".

During all the years I traveled with this man, I never really understood how he was able to do all the things he did. Magic seemed to be out of the question because the things he did were usually done before our very eyes, and one of the twelve of us would surely have seen any trickery he used. Maybe he was possessed, no, because if he were possessed there would be no good to come out of his actions. I truly could not understand his powers, so as time went on, I just came to know my friend as a very unique man, one who was able to do many things, such as healing the sick, or feeding the hungry, and most of all, loving and caring for all he met. Deep down inside I began to want to be like him, but how could I be? I was too much of a skeptic.

As the years went on, and I traveled with this man, some of my skepticism were off. The more I saw my friend do with all the crowds that followed him, the easier it was for me to accept him for who he was, he truly was a special man. I finally began to relinquish some of the doubts I had about this man. After all these years, the acts he performed could not come from any power here on earth. Where did my friend come from, what was his purpose to be here? Soon I would find out.

After a few years of being with this man, things began to change, it all started at a river called The Jordan. There was a man there dipping people in the river, a ritual he called baptism, then a strange thing happened. My friend stepped into the water to be baptized, and when he came up out of the water, a voice from above said, "This is my beloved son in whom I am well pleased." Now this voice not only scared me, but it brought back my skepticism. Sure, I had seen all the things my friend had done over the years, but to hear these words which sounded like that of a father come out of nowhere, I was confused. Now, as we continued to travel from city to city, my friend continued to draw numerous crowds to hear him speak, but then when he went home, things changed drastically. His first day back was like his hometown had been waiting for him to return all these years. The town seemed to recognize him as a king, and welcomed him home with a parade and joyous shouts, but this was to be short lived. The leaders of the city were angered by all the attention he was receiving, and this proved to be my friend's downfall, so it seemed. My friend was soon accused falsely of wrongdoings, and was sent before the ruler of the land to determine what punishment he should receive. The ruler saw no real evidence of what my friend had done wrong, so he put the verdict on the crowd in the courtyard, to which they shouted, "Crucify him!, crucify him," and so the sentence was handed down. My friend was hung on a cross to die, but this was not to be the end, but rather, the beginning, and soon I would understand what he meant when he told us, " In three days, I will rebuild my temple."

It was now the third day after my friends death, and we received word that my friends body had been stolen from the tomb. Sadness overtook us when we heard the news. Two of my friends went to see if it was true, and on their way, they ran into a woman who told them, He is alive, he is alive! My friends were overjoyed with the news and brought it back to us, but my scientific mind came back to me, and I did not believe them. No one could come back from the dead.

Well, I'm not sure where I was on that particular night, but my friend came and had dinner with the rest of my friends. I had missed all the excitement of seeing the man who had been our leader for so many years. All of my friends found me and told me that our leader was alive, but I being the stubborn person I was, said, "I'll believe it when I see his hands and his feet."

Finally, it was a couple of days later and we were having our supper, and our friend appeared out of nowhere. He came straight to me and told me to look at his hands, and to put my hand in his side. "It truly is you master," I said. "You have believed because you have seen, blessed are those who have not seen, and still believe." I was so embarrassed. I am no longer the skeptic I used to be.

Only A Father's Love
Home
Home
Will you marry me
No
Welcome Home!

ONLY A
FATHER'S LOVE

"Get up, get up, and go help your brother take care of the fields," I heard my father say. Something about this day seemed different, and indeed, it would be. I'd heard these words from my father so many times, but this morning, I just snapped.

Father, I'm leaving! I can't take it anymore, every morning it's the same old thing from you, and then I hear it from my brother Daniel also. "Get to work, finish plowing the field," do this, do that, I've had it father, I'm leaving. Can I get my inheritance now? You will never see me again. Again I told him, I can't take it around here anymore. With tears in his eyes, my father gave me all that was mine, and as I was leaving, he said, "I love you son, and remember, you will always have a home here." We hugged, and I was on my way.

Wow! Freedom! No more chores, no one to tell me what to do. I have plenty of money, now I can enjoy life on my own, I am free! As I left home, I wondered, what will I do first, where will I go?

I decided to go to my friend's houses, but to my dismay, they were still doing their chores. Can't you just come and celebrate with me? After all, now I was free, and I wanted to celebrate, have a party, but all my friends rejected my invitations. It was so disappointing, could they not be happy with me for just one day? Well alright, I'll just go into town and make some new friends.

As I walked into town, it wasn't the same as it was when I was with Daniel and my father, it was like no one knew me without them. So many times I had come into town before, how could they not know me? Well, no matter what, I wasn't going back home, so I better find a place to live. I searched through town an found nothing, so on to the next town, and the next. Finally, just before dusk, I found a place for 50 Dinari a month, it was about 35 kilometers from home.

By now the marketplace was closed, so I had no dinner tonight, but that was ok, I'll just go to sleep and go shopping in the morning. I could not sleep, my stomach was growling louder than a lion, and I thought to myself how Daniel was probably fast asleep, his stomach all full, and not growling. How nice that would be right now I thought, and then I remembered why I had left home, was it worth it? Yes, I told myself, I'll just go to the store in the morning, and all will be fine.

After a restless night, morning finally came. When I got to the store, I got a rude awakening, groceries were not cheap. Not to worry I told myself, I had plenty of money. Now that I had a full stomach again, I headed back into town to make some new friends, have fun, and enjoy life. I met a man and he invited me to join him to go to one of the game halls in town. We went in and sat around a table where five or six were playing a game. While I watched my friend and the other players, I saw them throwing money into a pot, and all of a sudden I heard my friend cry out, "I won," and I watched as he took the pot of money. Wow! My friend had just got a bunch of money, just by playing a game, and that's all it took for me, I was in, neglecting to see what the other six players had lost. I joined in the games, and although I did lose some games, I won more, and so this became a source of income.

One night on the way home, feeling kind of lonely, I met a woman on the street, and invited her to come to my house. We talked for awhile, and soon I fell in love with her, but when I asked her to marry me, she said, "No." Now I was confused, we had been together for a few months now and I thought she felt the same about me, but now it appeared that she just wanted my money. What was I going to do now? She had taken most of my money, and what was left, I gambled away, feeling sure I would win the pot again. I never did.

Broke, hungry, and a week to go on my little shack's rent, I was desperate, I had to find work. Finally, I got a job, the lowest in my culture, feeding the swine and cleaning their pens. This job paid just enough money to eat with, so now I had no more home. It was so humiliating, not only was I feeding and cleaning up after the pigs, now I was living with them.

It had been a year since I left my father's house, and as I thought about it, I thought about my brother Daniel, and my friends. They were all in nice warm houses, and here I was, freezing, trying to keep warm cuddling up with the pigs. Had my freedom from my chores, or Daniel constantly telling me to get back to work, really been worth this so called freedom I now had? The two did not match up, so I decided to try to beg my father to let me come live in his home again as a servant.

The day's journey was a long one, but finally, I got to my father's property. There was Daniel, plowing the field, had I put a toll on him by leaving? I felt bad. Then down the road I saw my father running towards me yelling, "My son, my son, you've come home." With tears in my eyes, I ran to him, saying over and over again, I'm sorry father, can I come back and live in your house as a servant? "Nonsense, you are my son, set up for a party," my father told the servants. Finally, Daniel came in from the fields, tired and sweaty. What was this, who for he thought, and then he saw me, and stormed out of the house. My father saw Daniel leave and ran after him. "Daniel, come back." As he turned around, he asked his father, "How does he deserve a party, am I not the one who has stayed and tended the chores, and continued to love you, despite everything he has done, how is this fair?" My father replied gently, "Daniel, be happy, your brother has come home, he was dead, and now he is alive! Everything I have is now yours alone. I love you son, please come in and rejoice with us." And so it was, I now had nothing, but yet I felt like I had everything,thanks to my father's love.

The Greatest Day of My Life

The Greatest Day of My Life

Hello, I am just a child, but I want to tell you about a day I will never forget, do you want to hear it? Well, hear it is.

First, let me tell you a little about myself. I am eight years old, my family consists of my parents, my sister, and of course, me. My father works very hard tending the sheep each day, while my mother stays home and takes care of our home. My mother cooks, cleans, and most of all, she takes care of my sister and me. We are a very loving family. On the Sabbath we go to the synagogue to worship. Well, enough about me.

For awhile now, we had heard about a very special man coming to visit our area. My parents were very excited to see this man, for they had heard so much about him, they wanted to see if he was as special as all their friends were saying.

The day of this man's arrival finally came, but my father had to tend our sheep, and my mother ended up having to stay home with my sister who was sick on this day. I felt so bad for my mother because she had waited so long for this day, and now she could not go, she was so disappointed, why did my sister have to be sick on this day, of all days?

I decided to go out and play with my friends as I always did after my chores were done. My friends and I were having a blast playing our favorite game, when in the distance we saw a huge crowd coming our way. What was with all of these people? We never had many crowds come to our town, and then I remembered, this was the day that special man was coming to town. Me and my friends continued to play as we watched all the people head for the lake where this man was to speak. I could play no longer as I thought about how disappointed my mother was at not being able to see this man, and that is when the thought came to my mind, maybe I could go and see this man and come home and tell my mother all about him. Yes! That is what I would do. I told my friends goodbye, and ran home to tell my mother my plan.

At first my mother was leery about my going, after all, I was only eight, but I told her it was only a short distance to the lake, and that there would be plenty of people I knew there. I'll be alright mother, please let me go so I can tell you about this man, so she finally agreed to let me go, but she insisted that I take a lunch, not knowing how long he would talk to us, so she gave me five loaves and two fish to take with me. "There, that should be enough for you, and if someone else did not bring a lunch, I think you will have enough to share, but be sure to be home by dark," Yes mother, I replied, as I hurried out the door.

As I arrived, there were so many people. Where had they all come from? I had never seen so many people. Since I was so small, I could not even see the man, so I just kept on squeezing my way through the crowd until I got to the front, and there he was! The smile on his face was so radiant, and his outstretched arms just seemed to say come, and be my friend, and then he began to speak. His voice was as gentle as my father's, and it was then that I realized how special this man was. He could have been anyone's father. As I listened to him speak, I just wanted to go up and give him a hug, just as I did every day with my own father. This man spoke about how we should love one another, and always be kind to each other, truly, there was something special about this man. Oh, how I wished my family could be here with me now, I was so grateful to my mother for letting me come. By now the crowd was starting to get hungry, for it had been a long afternoon, and this man suggested to his followers that we all be fed. His followers said to him, "We do not have enough food for this crowd, and the markets will all be closed at this hour, what should we do?" The man then asked if anyone had brought a lunch, and my hand just shot up, I remembered my mother's words about sharing my lunch, but what was to come now, I shall never forget. I only have five loaves and two fish, I replied, but you can have them. His followers just laughed, "that lunch will barely feed him, let alone, this whole crowd." The man took my lunch, and after he prayed, he handed my five loaves and two fish to his followers and told them to feed the crowd. His followers did as they were told, and to my amazement, everyone had been fed, and there were still baskets left over. I had just witnessed why this man was so special. He was miraculous!

I finally arrived home, exhausted from all had seen this day, not to mention from having to carry a basket of food home. "Where did you get all that food from," my mother asked? I told her what had happened, and how I had remembered her words about sharing my lunch. My mother just started crying, saying, "I am so proud of you son." I just hugged her with all my might and said, I Love you mother! This truly was the greatest day of my life.

MAY I HELP YOU

There I was, lying on the side of the road, gasping for what might be my last breath, shedding my last tears, as I was now ready to die from the injuries I had received.

It had been a particularly long day that day, business had done well, and then as I was on my way home to tell my family about the wonderful day I had been blessed with, it happened. The route home was not my normal route home, and I knew better than to take this route, but because of the successful day it was, and the money I was carrying, I chose to take a less traveled route in the hope that it would be safer. On this day, it was not, and I almost lost my life because of my choice, but thanks to one person, I can tell you my story.

The sun was nearly down, this route seemed to be taking longer than I had remembered on previous trips, but oh well, I had to get home, not too much farther to go, and then they came. Bandits, thieves, nomads, whatever you want to call them, I was attacked, robbed, beaten, and left for dead. Why had I taken this route I asked myself, why was I so stupid? I knew the risk of taking this route home, and what good did it do me now, as I was just waiting to die. No joyful and exciting news to tell my family now, if I ever got to see them again, was it really worth the risk? Over and over again, I kept asking myself.

Wow! I think I see someone coming, will they help me, I wondered? I could not stand, so I just raised my hand and tried to yell for help, but all I heard as he passed on the other side of the road was, "Don't bother me, I must get to my meeting in the synagogue." Must have been a pharisee or someone important I thought to myself, but why would he not help me? Now I could barely see the sun peeking over the horizon, as it prepared to go to sleep for the night, and to my amazement, I saw another figure coming towards me, and once again I felt sure that this man would stop and help me, but again he, in his nice clothes, just passed me by saying, "Leave me alone, I must get home." My heart sank, I knew that two people were more than what should have been on this route on any given day, so I just put my arm down, and continued to wait for my last breath to come. By now I had no more tears to shed, so I just closed my eyes to die.

By now it was dark, pitch black, my life was over, or so I thought. Oh no! Not again I thought as I was kicked again. I started to scream, No! No! Not again, and then I heard a kind and gentle voice say, "I'm sorry, I did not see you, are you alright? May I help you?" My voice was next to nothing by now, but with as much as I could get out, I just said, please help me. His gestures were so subtle as he carefully picked me up, and put me on his donkey. The pain was unbearable, but I decided to try to hold onto my life, maybe I would see my family again. Where are you from, what is your name, I asked. "Please, just rest, I will get you help soon," and that he did. Meanwhile, the trip to the next town seemed to take forever, but we finally made it, and thank goodness, there was still one inn with a candle burning in the window. This man carried me in, got me a room, and told the inn keeper to take care of me, and whatever the costs were, he would take care of them on his next trip into town. Thank you was nowhere near enough for what this man had done for me, but I offered it anyway. "No problem, your dept will be paid in full," were his last words to me.

I never learned the man's name, but I do recall him saying he was from Samaria. Why had he stopped? His country and ours did not get along, we were enemies. My only thought was that he must have been sent by an angel to help me, and he did. As a result of this man's help, when he did not have to, I can tell you my story of how, on a lonely road so long ago, my life was changed because of one man who who did not have to help me, asked, "May I help you?" A life was changed that day, and now I am always willing to ask, May I help you, no matter who they might be.

He Is Real

HE IS REAL

Hello, my name is Martha, and I would like to tell you about the greatest man who ever lived, in my opinion. This man had come to visit us whenever he was in town. He was a kind and gentle man, and my sister and I always enjoyed his visits, we always welcomed him into our home. My sister and I were two different people, me always worrying about appearances, and Mary, was a very caring and compassionate woman. I'm not saying that I don't have compassion, because I do, it is just not a priority with me, as it is with Mary.

Let me give you an example of the two of us. One day our friend came to visit us, and 1, just being me, busied myself cleaning the house to make it spotless for our guest, and what was Mary doing, she was just sitting at the man's feet, washing them. Of course, I was a little put out by Mary's actions. I felt she should be helping me clean, but this man told me to leave my sister alone, for she was doing what needed to be done also, according to the culture of our land. In our land, we only wore sandals, or nothing on our feet, so when guests came, we would offer to wash their feet. Well, this was how Mary and I were different, but where we were alike, was in the belief that our friend was unique, he was able to do things we had never seen any other man do, and one day, it happened to us.

Mary and I came home one day and found our brother Lazarus dead. How could this be? He was our brother, he was not supposed to die yet. We were so distraught and broken up, our brother was truly dead, so we buried him. Well, it just so happened that our friend, who was able to do such great things, was coming into town, so Mary and I talked together, and we decided to see if this man could save our brother. I left Mary at home, and I set out to find our friend and bring him home with me, in hope's that he could bring our brother back to life. We did not know if he could, but we believed in him. In my state of anxiety when i saw him, I told him, if you had been here, Lazarus would not have died. I was in tears, and then, this man knowing our brother also, began to cry, and that is when I knew he was real. He had compassion in his heart, just as Mary and I did. Our friends were also amazed, we could not understand how or why this man, who we considered to be the greatest man on earth, would shed tears. We were astounded!

This man asked us to take him to our brother's burial place, so we did. He told us to roll away the stone in front of his tomb, and me, being Martha, told this man that he had been in the grave for four days now, and he was going to stink. What was I thinking? This man was coming to possibly save my brother's life, and all I could think about, was how bad he was going to smell.

It was now that this man prayed for all of us to see, that he believed in a higher power also, and after his prayer of thanks, he told Lazarus to come out of the grave, and he did! Our brother was alive again! All we could do was thank this man for the compassion he showed to us. This man was REAL, and truly, the greatest man ever!

Printed in the United States
By Bookmasters